Brer Rabbit TRICKING

Sean Taylor

Illustrated by
Dave McTaggart

OXFORD

OXFORD

UNIVERSITY PRESS

Great Clarendon Street, Oxford OX2 6DP

Oxford University Press is a department of the University of Oxford.
It furthers the University's objective of excellence in research, scholarship,
and education by publishing worldwide in

Oxford New York

Auckland Bangkok Buenos Aires Cape Town Chennai
Dar es Salaam Delhi Hong Kong Istanbul Karachi Kolkata
Kuala Lumpur Madrid Melbourne Mexico City Mumbai Nairobi
São Paulo Shanghai Taipei Tokyo Toronto

with an associated company in Berlin

Oxford is a registered trade mark of Oxford University Press
in the UK and in certain other countries

Illustrated by Dave McTaggart © 2002

First published 2002

British Library Cataloguing in Publication Data

Data available

ISBN 0 19 919494 7

1 3 5 7 9 10 8 6 4 2

Guided Reading Pack (6 of the same title): ISBN 0 19 919573 0
Mixed Pack (1 of 6 different titles): ISBN 0 19 919499 8
Class Pack (6 copies of 6 titles): ISBN 0 19 919500 5

Printed in Hong Kong

Contents

CLICK!!

Chapter 1

Brer Rabbit's Trickbag

Some people call him Brother Rabbit. Some people shorten the name to Brer Rabbit. But, whatever you call him, you can be sure that he is the cleverest animal in the world.

And Brer Rabbit is not only clever. He is clever in a tricky kind of way.

He is not only clever in a tricky kind of way. He is funny in a clever, tricky kind of way. Which is why he is forever pestering the other animals, playing jokes and making mischief.

Brer Rabbit's neighbour, Brer Fox, knows all about those jokes. In fact, he was the one who opened Brer Rabbit's trickbag.

It all started one day when Brer Fox
was walking down the big road. As he
strolled along, he happened to spot
Brer Terrapin. That made Brer Fox give
a chuckle, down in his red belly.

"Heh-heh-heh," he went.

Then he slipped into the shadows,
with his small eyes fixed on Brer
Terrapin's leathery little head.

Brer Terrapin waddled slowly up the road, humming quietly to himself. As he came past, Brer Fox pounced and flipped him into a sack.

Then he slung the sack across his back and headed home.

Brer Terrapin yelled out and struggled about, but Brer Fox didn't pay any attention.

"I'm going to boil him up," he said, "Nothing tastes as good as a hot pot of terrapin stew."

But, if you had looked very carefully into the bushes up the road, you would have seen two, long, brown ears.

Below those ears you would have seen a pair of eyes as dark and soft as velvet. It was Brer Rabbit.

He was lying beside the road, kicking at the butterflies and nibbling at the grass stalks.

As Brer Fox came past, his ears pricked up and he looked out through the leaves.

"Now I wonder what that old rascal's got in that sack?" Brer Rabbit asked himself. And he decided that there would be no harm in going to find out. So off he went.

He took a short cut along the ditch,
over the turnip field and through the
bramble patch.

That way, he got to Brer Fox's house
first.

Before long, Brer Fox came home
and, as soon as he opened the door,
Brer Rabbit poked his head through
the window. He pretended to be in an
awful panic.

"Brer Fox! Brer Fox!" he called.

"What?" asked Brer Fox, giving a jump.

"Your watermelon patch!" gasped Brer Rabbit. "Somebody's up there trampling on everything! I tried to stop them but they wouldn't listen! Hurry up if you want to catch them!"

"What? Not my juicy watermelons?" cried Brer Fox. "Thanks for telling me, Brer Rabbit."

He dropped his sack in the corner and scurried off to his watermelon patch as fast as his skinny legs could carry him.

Brer Rabbit's beady eyes looked right, then left. Then he hopped in through the window, as quietly as a cat.

Once inside, he picked up the sack.

"Ouch!" squeaked a voice from inside. "Let me out! Let me go! Ow! Ouch!"

Brer Rabbit jumped back in surprise.
Then he said, "There's only one animal
around here who squeaks as loud as
that. It's Brer Terrapin."

With that, he reached in and pulled
his old friend out of the sack.

"Brer Rabbit!" squeaked Brer
Terrapin. "Help me! Brer Fox is
going to boil me into a hot pot of
terrapin soup!"

"Okey-dokey," said Brer Rabbit, wondering what to do. Then he gave a little smile. He'd had an idea.

He carried Brer Terrapin up into the woods where he would be safe and sound.

Next he hunted around in the trees until he found what he was looking for.

Then he went back to Brer Fox's house with the sack. He was very careful with that sack.

There was something in it, just the same size as Brer Terrapin. But it wasn't Brer Terrapin.

Brer Rabbit laid it gently in the corner of Brer Fox's room. Then he skipped and hopped back up to the woods and sat down beside Brer Terrapin.

It was only a minute or two before Brer Fox was back, panting and grumbling. He hadn't found anyone in his watermelon patch.

"That Brer Rabbit," he muttered. "One more trick and I'm going to skin him alive!"

He pushed open the door and he smiled. His bag was just where he had left it.

"Well, that's all right," he nodded, reaching for his cooking pot. "Now where was I?" He picked up his bag.

Moments later, there was a crash as if a cooking pot had been thrown at the ceiling.

This was followed by a banging and a whooping that was so loud the chimney wobbled on the rooftop. It sounded as though a herd of cows was running through the place.

Brer Rabbit and Brer Terrapin could hear chairs being thrown around and plates being smashed.

Then the door flew open. Out came Brer Fox with his ears flat on his head and a swarm of wasps after him.

"You put a wasps' nest in the sack!" squeaked Brer Terrapin.

"I suppose I must have done!" said Brer Rabbit, with a giggle.

Brer Fox ran yelping down the path towards the pond.

When he got to the water, he splashed in head first. That made Brer Rabbit shake with laughter so much that Brer Terrapin couldn't help joining in.

"Don't, Brer Rabbit! Don't!" squeaked Brer Terrapin, clutching his stomach.

Brer Rabbit tried to control himself.

But then Brer Fox came sneezing and sloshing out of the pond with a twirl of duckweed tangled round his ears.

And that made the two friends burst out laughing again. They rolled around, shaking their heads and kicking up the leaves.

"Right!" spluttered Brer Fox, swishing his soggy tail from side to side. "That skinny little floppy-eared pinhead Brer Rabbit has HAD IT!"

Chapter 2

Poor Brer Fox is Dead

Brer Fox was so angry with Brer Rabbit that he hardly knew which way to turn.

"I've got to find a way to catch him," he muttered. "Then he'll see! I'll have his skin for sausages!"

And the thought of it made him give a chuckle, down in his red belly.

"Heh-heh-heh!"

Then, who should he see coming past his house but his friend, Brer Wolf.

"How are you, Brer Wolf?" he called through the window.

"I'm fine," said Brer Wolf, smiling with his big teeth.

Brer Wolf stopped to chat and Brer Fox told him all about Brer Rabbit's trick with the wasps' nest.

"It's time we caught that Brer
Rabbit," said Brer Wolf. "And I've got a
clever idea. We'll get him into your
house. Then we can grab him."

"But how are we going to get him
into my house?" asked Brer Fox.

"We're going to fool him in," said
Brer Wolf.

"And who's going to do the fooling?"

"Leave the fooling to me," said Brer Wolf. "All you need to do is get into bed and pretend to be dead."

"What's Brer Wolf up to?" Brer Fox wondered. "Something clever, I'll bet. Because he's just about the cleverest animal around here."

Then Brer Fox lay down and pretended to be dead.

Meanwhile, Brer Wolf was already knocking on Brer Rabbit's door,

"BLAM! BLAM! BLAM!"

Brer Rabbit peeped out and saw that it was Brer Wolf. He blinked his dark eyes.

"Open the door, Brer Rabbit," said Brer Wolf.

"I don't have time," Brer Rabbit replied.

"It's important," said Brer Wolf.

"What I'm doing is important, too."

"This is a matter of life and death!" said Brer Wolf.

Well, Brer Rabbit didn't have much choice.

"Okey-dokey," he said. "I'll open the door a crack. But don't come anywhere near me. I've just come down with a terrible attack of fleas."

With that, the door creaked open a crack and Brer Wolf's grey eyes peered inside.

"I've got some awfully sad news, Brer Rabbit," he said, putting his hand on his heart. "Poor Brer Fox is dead. He's lying on the bed up at his house, as dead as a dodo."

Brer Rabbit looked at Brer Wolf's serious face and asked himself, "Now, is he tricking me or not?"

Brer Rabbit couldn't help feeling curious. So he told Brer Wolf he was sorry to hear the news. And he decided to go up the road to Brer Fox's place, just to see what was what.

When he got there, everything was quiet. He pushed open the door, just a little.

Then he looked inside. Sure enough, there was Brer Fox, stretched out on the bed with his eyes shut.

So Brer Rabbit walked in.

"Well, I'll be blessed," said Brer Rabbit in his saddest voice. "Poor Brer Fox is dead. At least, he looks as if he's dead. But maybe he isn't. Because I've heard that whenever a visitor comes to see a dead body, the dead body lifts up its hind legs and shouts WAHOO!"

There was a moment's silence. Then Brer Fox lifted up his hind legs and shouted, "WAHOO!"

Brer Rabbit shook his head, as if he felt sorry for Brer Fox for being such a fool. Then he called out, "So long, neighbour!"

And he shot out of the house, leaving Brer Fox with his skinny legs still sticking up in the air.

Brer Fox slowly opened his eyes and sat up. He knew that he'd been outwitted again. And he put his hand on his jaw like someone with a painful toothache.

"That fluffy-tailed, flea-bitten little blabbermouth!" he muttered. "If he thinks he's ever going to trick me again, he's wrong by about a thousand miles!"

Brer Rabbit, meanwhile, was almost home. As he ran down the middle of the road, he kicked his legs up in the air and shouted, "WAHOO!"

Chapter 3

Quicksand!

Soon, the weather changed for the worse. It was cold. It was wet. It was windy. Winter had arrived and that meant there would be hard times for a few weeks.

There was nothing much to eat and many of the animals went to bed hungry. But Brer Rabbit didn't let that stop him traipsing around and getting into frolics.

One day he noticed something strange. Although all his friends were getting thinner and thinner, Brer Wolf was getting fatter and fatter. That bothered Brer Rabbit.

"Here we are so hungry that our ribs are showing!" he said to himself. "And Brer Wolf's looking as fat as a ball of butter. Something's up."

So he kept an eye on Brer Wolf and, before long, he found out what was going on. Brer Wolf was stealing chickens from Mr Man's farm.

Then, every week, he went to the market on his old horse-cart with a bag full of chickens to sell.

That way, he always had enough money to buy food.

So, the next market day, Brer Rabbit woke up before sunrise and set off walking towards town.

Before very long, Brer Wolf came past on his horse-cart, with a bag full of chickens on the back.

"'Morning Brer Rabbit," he said. "How are you?"

"Not so good," replied Brer Rabbit, wiping his brow. "I've got to go to the market to buy myself a new pocket hanky and it's an awfully long walk."

"Mmm …" said Brer Wolf, widening his stony eyes, "I'm going to the market myself."

"Oh, are you?" beamed Brer Rabbit. "Can I have a lift?"

"You're more than welcome," said Brer Wolf, feeling that his chance to catch Brer Rabbit had come at last.

Brer Rabbit jumped up on to the old horse-cart, and off they went.

Great, grey clouds were blowing
across the sky and it was bitterly cold.
The sun was only just starting to peep
through the trees.

After a time, Brer Wolf said,
"Brer Rabbit, I'm freezing! I'm so
cold I don't
know what
to do."

"There's a big fire across there in the
woods, Brer Wolf," said Brer Rabbit,
looking into the trees with his velvety
eyes. "You could go and warm yourself
beside it. And, since you've been so
kind, giving me a lift, I'll wait here with
the horse-cart."

Brer Wolf looked at the red glow
of the sun through the trees and
he thought that it was a fire.

"That's a good idea," he said.

He jumped down and went swishing
off through the wet leaves towards the
sunrise.

As soon as he had gone, Brer Rabbit
hopped off the cart, and cut the tails
off the horses. He hid the horses and
cart in some bushes.

Then he stuck the tails down deep in
the mud and stood holding them.

After a while, Brer Wolf came back
huffing and puffing.

"Did you warm yourself up?" asked
Brer Rabbit.

"No!" panted Brer Wolf. "That was a
very strange sort of fire, Brer Rabbit. I
ran and I ran, but the closer I got to it,
the further away it was!"

"Well," shrugged Brer Rabbit. "I had worse luck than you. Look! The horses got restless and ran off into this quicksand. The cart sank altogether. Luckily, I managed to grab hold of the horses' tails before they disappeared."

"My old horse-cart!" groaned Brer Wolf. "My chickens!"

"Never mind about them!" said Brer Rabbit. "Grab hold of one of these tails and pull, or you'll lose your horses as well!"

Wolf grabbed hold of a tail
wo of them pulled.
nk mine's coming!" said Brer
gritting his teeth.

"So's mine!" said Brer Rabbit.

Suddenly, both the tails came flying
out of the mud.

Brer Wolf looked down at the tails.

Then he looked across at Brer
Rabbit. Brer Rabbit scratched his head.
"Well I never!" he said. "We pulled so
hard that their tails came right off!"

For a moment Brer Wolf looked as
if he'd been hit on the head with a
frying pan.

He hung around for a few minutes,
peering down into the mud.

But, what with the cold wind, it wasn't very long before he gave up and went home.

Brer Rabbit waited until he was out of earshot.

Then he got the horse-cart out of the bushes, and drove it away with the bag full of chickens still on the back.

When he got home, he invited all of his friends round for a party. Brer Terrapin came, Brer Raccoon, Sister Cow, little Mr Cricket, Brer Billy Goat and Mr Benjamin Ram. They danced so much that they nearly fell through the floorboards.

Brer Rabbit's wife cooked the chickens, and that night none of them went to bed hungry.

Chapter 4

Old Man Spewter-Splutter

The next morning, the sun came out.
Brer Wolf threw open his curtains,
and what should he see but his old
horse-cart standing outside his house?
But no bag of chickens on the back.

It didn't take him very long to work
out what had happened.

"That mangy little rabbit-brained muppet, Brer Rabbit!" he growled. With a face like thunder, he set off up the road towards Brer Fox's house.

When Brer Rabbit woke up, he felt just fine.

His wife said that since the sun had come out, he ought go down to the hardware shop to buy some things for the family.

"What do we need?" asked Brer Rabbit.

"Seven tin cups for the children to drink from," said his wife. "Seven tin plates for them to eat off. And a new coffee-pot to put on the stove."

"Okey-dokey," said Brer Rabbit.

He skipped off down the big road towards the hardware shop. And he whistled up at the birds when he spotted them circling in the blue sky.

But he didn't spot the small eyes of
Brer Fox and the grey eyes of Brer Wolf,
watching him from the woods.

"He must be going to the hardware
shop," blinked Brer Fox.

"Well, that's just fine," said Brer
Wolf, snapping his big teeth together.
"Let's arrange a little surprise for him."

Brer Fox nodded and gave a chuckle,
down in his red belly.

"Heh-heh-heh!"

The two of them headed off through the woods towards the home of their old friend, Brer Bear.

It was a long, dusty walk to the hardware shop. Brer Rabbit bought the tin cups, he bought the tin plates and he bought the coffee-pot to put on the stove.

Then he headed home. But the walk back was no shorter than the walk there. And, when he got to the steep hill between the cornfields, he was feeling pretty tired. So he sat down by the side of the road to catch his breath.

Now, as he was sitting there, he
noticed some prints in the sand.
Someone had been there only a short
while before.

He scratched his head and
looked a little closer at
the marks in
the sand.

One was the print of something with
a long, bushy tail. Beside it was the
print of something with a long, thin
tail. And beside that was a great, big,
round print of something that didn't
have a tail at all.

Brer Rabbit knew full well who those tails belonged to. And he knew who had left the big, round print as well.

"Brer Fox and Brer Wolf are playing smart, are they?" he said to himself.

"They've come up here to lay a trap for me. And they've brought Brer Bear along with them, too. It won't be the first time they've tried it. And it won't be the first time I get them before they get me."

He sneaked off into the bushes, away from the road, and up to the top of the hill. From the hilltop he could look down on everything for miles around.

Sure enough, there they were, hiding down in the cornfields.

Brer Wolf was on one side of the road with his ears pricked up. Brer Fox was on the other side of the road, scratching his nose. And Brer Bear was lying in the ditch, having a nap.

Brer Rabbit knew at once what he was going to do. And he liked the idea so much that he did a little dance round and round. He had to put a paw over his mouth to stop himself from laughing.

First, he turned the coffee-pot upside down and stuck it on his head.

Next, he ran his belt through the handles of the tin cups, so that they were hanging round his waïst.

Then he picked up a tin plate in each
hand and set off running down the hill.

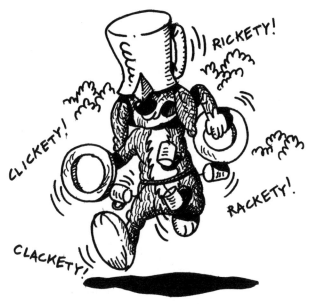

"Clickety, rickety, rackety, clackety!"
went the cups round his waist as he
gathered speed.

Brer Fox and Brer Wolf looked
around and saw the strangest looking
creature racing towards them. They had
never seen anything like it before. It
had huge shiny hands and a great long
beak.

The two animals hopped out on to the road with eyes as wide as windows.

"CLICKETY, RICKETY, RACKETY, CLACKETY!" went the cups round Brer Rabbit's waist. "SLAMBANG!" went the plates, as he smashed them together like a pair of cymbals.

That woke up Brer Bear. He saw the savage thing hurtling towards him, and he panicked. He stumbled up on to the road and crashed into Brer Wolf.

"I'm a wolf! Don't push me! Don't push me!" yelled Brer Wolf, as Brer Rabbit bounded through the bushes towards them.

"I'm a fox …" said Brer Fox, but, before he could say anything else, Brer Rabbit leapt out of the bushes and on to the road.

For a moment, Brer Bear looked as though he was going to protect his smaller friends. But Brer Rabbit slapped the plates together again and came leaping along the middle of the road.

"Gimme room! Turn me loose! I'm Old Man Spewter-Splutter with long claws and scales on my back! I'm snaggle-toothed and double-jointed! GIMME ROOM! GIMME ROOM!"

And Brer Bear ran off so fast that he brought down a whole section of the fence around the cornfield.

Meanwhile, Brer Fox and Brer Wolf hoisted up their tails and shot off so fast that they nearly ran past their own shadows.

"SLAMBANG!" went Brer Rabbit's tin plates one more time, just to see them off.

None of the animals turned round until they were right the way across the cornfield. And, when they did look back, who should they see but Brer Rabbit.

He was shaking his ears out of the coffee-pot and quivering with the giggles.

Brer Fox, Brer Wolf and Brer Bear hardly knew how to control themselves. But Brer Rabbit didn't bother. He fell down by the side of the road, kicked up his heels and laughed until he couldn't laugh any more.

Brer Fox was after him. Brer Wolf was after him. Brer Bear was after him, too.

But they haven't caught him yet ...

About the author

I was born in England, but now spend a lot of time in Brazil.

Throughout the world you will find tales about Brer Rabbit the "trickster" – someone who can "wheedle the whiskers of a thistle".

The Brer Rabbit stories were told by African-American storytellers and written down by Joel Chandler Harris. Re-telling the stories was, to quote him, "a monstrous gigglement".